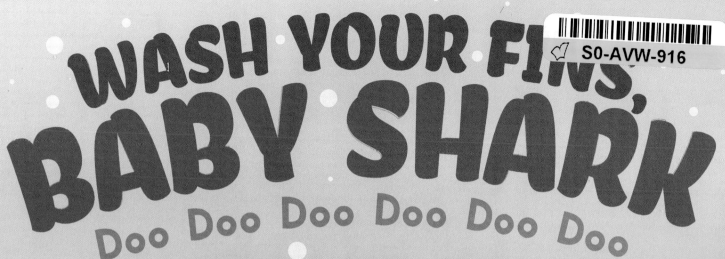

WASH YOUR FINS, BABY SHARK
Doo Doo Doo Doo Doo Doo

LÁVATE LAS ALETAS, BEBÉ TIBURÓN
Duu Duu Duu Duu Duu Duu

Art by / Arte de
John John Bajet

ISBN 978-1-338-72306-9

10 9 8 7 6 5 4 3 2 1   20 21 22 23 24

Printed in U.S.A.   40
First bilingual printing, 2020
Designed by Doan Buu

On your own or with your siblings in tow,
Washing your hands is the way to go.
BABY SHARK knows how fun it can be.
Let's wash our fins under the sea!

Solo o con tus hermanitos,
Lavarte las manos es lo debido.
BEBÉ TIBURÓN lo sabe disfrutar.
¡Lavémonos las aletas bajo el mar!

Wash your fins, doo doo doo doo doo doo.
Wash your fins, doo doo doo doo doo doo.

Lávate las aletas, duu duu duu duu duu duu.
Lávate las aletas, duu duu duu duu duu duu.

Wash your fins, doo doo doo doo doo doo.
WASH YOUR FINS!
Lávate las aletas, duu duu duu duu duu duu.
¡LÁVATE LAS ALETAS!

Water on, doo doo doo doo doo doo.
Water on, doo doo doo doo doo doo.

Abre la llave, duu duu duu duu duu duu.
Abre la llave, duu duu duu duu duu duu.

Water on, doo doo doo doo doo doo.
WATER ON!

Abre la llave, duu duu duu duu duu duu.
¡ABRE LA LLAVE!

Squirt the soap, doo doo doo doo doo doo.
Squirt the soap, doo doo doo doo doo doo.

Echa el jabón, duu duu duu duu duu duu.
Echa el jabón, duu duu duu duu duu duu.

Squirt the soap, doo doo doo doo doo doo.
SQUIRT THE SOAP!
Echa el jabón, duu duu duu duu duu duu.
¡ECHA EL JABÓN!

Lather up, doo doo doo doo doo doo.
Lather up, doo doo doo doo doo doo.

Haz espuma, duu duu duu duu duu duu.
Haz espuma, duu duu duu duu duu duu.

Lather up, doo doo doo doo doo doo.
LATHER UP!

Haz espuma, duu duu duu duu duu duu duu.
¡HAZ ESPUMA!

Scrub a dub, doo doo doo doo doo doo.

Restriégate bien, duu duu duu duu duu duu.

Scrub a dub, doo doo doo doo doo doo.

SCRUB A DUB!

Restriégate bien, duu duu duu duu duu duu.

¡RESTRIÉGATE BIEN!

Sing and wash, doo doo doo doo doo doo.
Sing and wash, doo doo doo doo doo doo.

Canta y lávate, duu duu duu duu duu duu.
Canta y lávate, duu duu duu duu duu duu.

Rinse those fins, doo doo doo doo doo.
Rinse those fins, doo doo doo doo doo doo.
Enjuágate las aletas, duu duu duu duu duu duu.
Enjuágate las aletas, duu duu duu duu duu duu.

Rinse those fins, doo doo doo doo doo doo.

RINSE THOSE FINS!

Enjuágate las aletas, duu duu duu duu duu duu.

¡ENJUÁGATE LAS ALETAS!

Dry them off, doo doo doo doo doo doo.
Dry them off, doo doo doo doo doo doo.
Sécatelas, duu duu duu duu duu duu.
Sécatelas, duu duu duu duu duu duu.

Dry them off, doo doo doo doo doo doo.
DRY THEM OFF!
Sécatelas, duu duu duu duu duu duu.
¡SÉCATELAS!

Nice and clean, doo doo doo doo doo doo.
Nice and clean, doo doo doo doo doo doo.

Bien limpiecito, duu duu duu duu duu duu.
Bien limpiecito, duu duu duu duu duu duu.

Nice and clean, doo doo doo doo doo doo.

NICE AND CLEAN!

Bien limpiecito, duu duu duu duu duu duu.

¡BIEN LIMPIECITO!

Teach your friends, doo doo doo doo doo doo.
Teach your friends, doo doo doo doo doo doo.
Teach your friends, doo doo doo doo doo doo.

Enseña a tus amigos, duu duu duu duu duu duu.
Enseña a tus amigos, duu duu duu duu duu duu.
Enseña a tus amigos, duu duu duu duu duu duu.

TEACH YOUR FRIENDS!
WASH YOUR FINS, BABY SHARK!
¡ESEÑA A TUS AMIGOS!
¡LÁVATE LAS ALETAS, BEBÉ TIBURÓN!

BABY SHARK'S HAND WASHING TIPS!
¡CONSEJOS DE BEBÉ TIBURÓN PARA LAVARSE LAS MANOS!

Washing your hands keeps you and the people around you healthy! Be sure to follow these tips:

¡Lavarse las manos los mantiene saludables a ti y a las personas a tu alrededor! Sigue estos consejos:

WASH
your hands often! Especially before eating food, after using the bathroom, and after you blow your nose, cough, or sneeze.

¡LÁVATE
las manos a menudo! Especialmente antes de comer, después de ir al baño y después de sonarte la nariz, toser o estornudar.

SCRUB
your hands for at least twenty seconds. Need a timer? Sing three verses of Baby Shark!

RESTRIÉGATE
bien las manos al menos durante veinte segundos. ¿Necesitas un cronómetro? ¡Canta tres estrofas de Bebé Tiburón!

LATHER
your hands and wrists with soap, and don't forget to wash between your fingers and under your nails.

ENJABÓNATE
las manos y las muñecas con mucho jabón y no olvides lavarte entre los dedos y debajo de las uñas.

DRY
your hands with a clean towel!

¡SÉCATE
las manos con una toalla limpia!

Washing your hands with soap and water is always best. But you can use an alcohol-based **HAND SANITIZER** if soap and water aren't available!

Siempre es mejor lavarse las manos con agua y jabón, ¡aunque también puedes usar un **DESINFECTANTE PARA MANOS** a base de alcohol si no hay agua y jabón disponibles!

Tips adapted from cdc.gov / Estos consejos han sido adaptados del sitio cdc.gov.